GULLIVER'S ADVENTURES IN LILLIPUT

by Jonathan Swift

Illustrated by
GENNADY SPIRIN

Retold by
Ann Keay Beneduce

PaperStar

The Putnam & Grosset Group

For my sons Ilya, Gennady, and Andrei
—G.S.

Printed on recycled paper

A PaperStar Book, published in 1996 by The Putnam & Grosset Group,
200 Madison Avenue, New York, NY 10016. PaperStar Books and
the PaperStar logo are trademarks of The Putnam Berkley Group, Inc.
Originally published in 1993 by Philomel Books.
Published simultaneously in Canada.
Printed in the United States of America.
Library of Congress Cataloging-in-Publication Data
Beneduce, Ann. Gulliver's adventures in Lilliput / by Jonathan Swift;
illustrated by Gennady Spirin; retold by Ann Keay Beneduce. p. cm.
Summary: An Englishman is shipwrecked in a land
where the people are only six inches tall.
[1. Fantasy.] I. Spirin, Gennady, ill.
II. Swift, Jonathan, 1667–1745. Gulliver's travels. III. Title.
PZ7.B43234Gu 1993 [E]—dc20 92-26200 CIP AC Rev
ISBN 0-698-11422-1
1 3 5 7 9 10 8 6 4 2

2

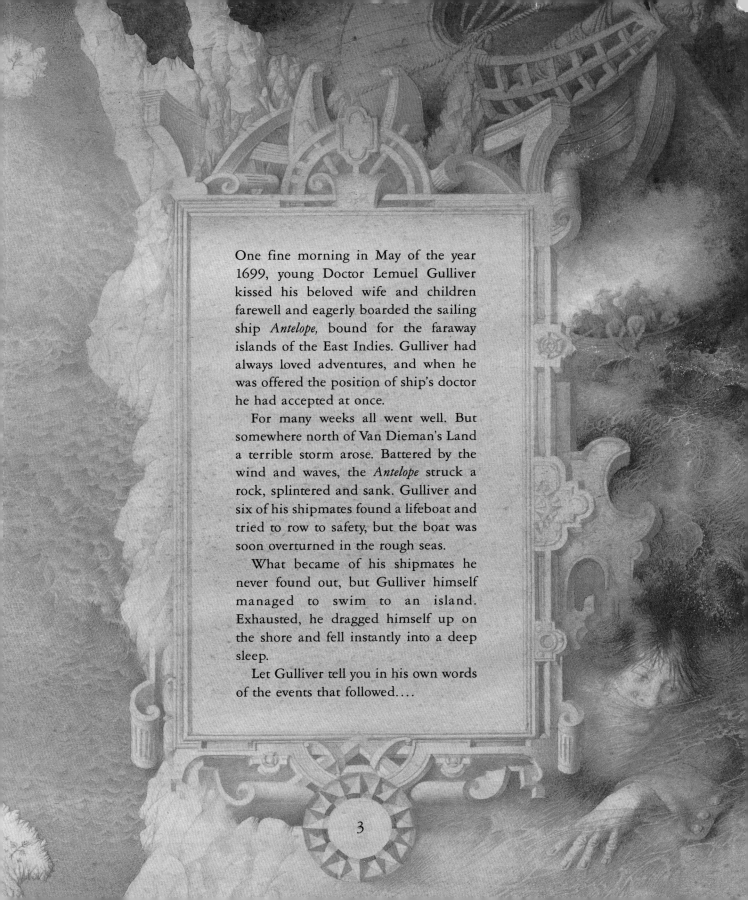

One fine morning in May of the year 1699, young Doctor Lemuel Gulliver kissed his beloved wife and children farewell and eagerly boarded the sailing ship *Antelope,* bound for the faraway islands of the East Indies. Gulliver had always loved adventures, and when he was offered the position of ship's doctor he had accepted at once.

For many weeks all went well. But somewhere north of Van Dieman's Land a terrible storm arose. Battered by the wind and waves, the *Antelope* struck a rock, splintered and sank. Gulliver and six of his shipmates found a lifeboat and tried to row to safety, but the boat was soon overturned in the rough seas.

What became of his shipmates he never found out, but Gulliver himself managed to swim to an island. Exhausted, he dragged himself up on the shore and fell instantly into a deep sleep.

Let Gulliver tell you in his own words of the events that followed....

I must have slept for a long time, for the sun had risen and shone quite high overhead when I awoke. I tried to stand up but found to my astonishment that I could not move. My hands and feet and even my hair seemed to be fastened down. Then I was horrified to feel some small animal creeping along my left leg and up to my chest. Straining to lift my head a little, I peered down and saw a tiny human creature not much bigger than my own middle finger. He was followed by about forty more of the same kind.

I was so surprised that I roared aloud. At this, they all ran back in fright and some even tumbled off. However, they soon came back and one climbed up to where he could get a full sight of my face.

"*Hekinah degul!*" he called out but, although I have studied several other languages beside my native English, I could not understand these words at all.

With a violent pull, I managed to break a few of the strings that bound my left hand. I then tried to catch some of the annoying little creatures, but they ran away too quickly. Then one of them cried out "*Tolgo phonac!*" In an instant I felt my left hand and my face pierced with hundreds of tiny arrows. I decided not to anger my small captors further. I lay still and tried to think about how to get them to set me free.

After a little while, I heard some knocking near my right ear and the sound of a great crowd. Turning my head as far as I could, I saw that some of the tiny people were building a tower about a foot and a half high. Now one little man, who seemed to be someone of importance, climbed up to the top of it and made a long speech, which I could not understand. He said the word *"Lilliput"* several times, however, and I guessed that this might be the name of the place I was in. He looked quite friendly and, since I was very hungry, I pointed to my mouth to indicate this. Before long, about a hundred inhabitants set ladders against my sides and climbed up and walked toward my mouth, carrying little baskets of food: miniature legs of lamb, tiny roasted turkeys or sides of beef. They were deliciously cooked, but three of them together made scarcely a mouthful for me.

Then someone called out, *"Peplum selam."* At this, they loosened the cords that bound me a little, so I was able to turn on my side. Before I knew it I was fast asleep. Only later did I discover that their doctors had put a sleeping potion into my food.

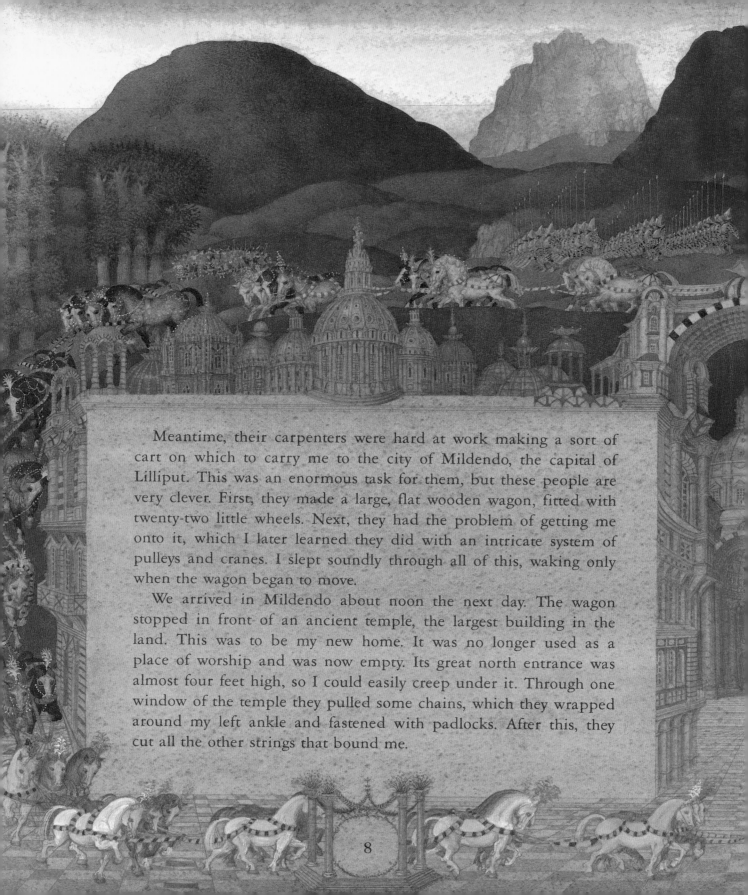

Meantime, their carpenters were hard at work making a sort of cart on which to carry me to the city of Mildendo, the capital of Lilliput. This was an enormous task for them, but these people are very clever. First, they made a large, flat wooden wagon, fitted with twenty-two little wheels. Next, they had the problem of getting me onto it, which I later learned they did with an intricate system of pulleys and cranes. I slept soundly through all of this, waking only when the wagon began to move.

We arrived in Mildendo about noon the next day. The wagon stopped in front of an ancient temple, the largest building in the land. This was to be my new home. It was no longer used as a place of worship and was now empty. Its great north entrance was almost four feet high, so I could easily creep under it. Through one window of the temple they pulled some chains, which they wrapped around my left ankle and fastened with padlocks. After this, they cut all the other strings that bound me.

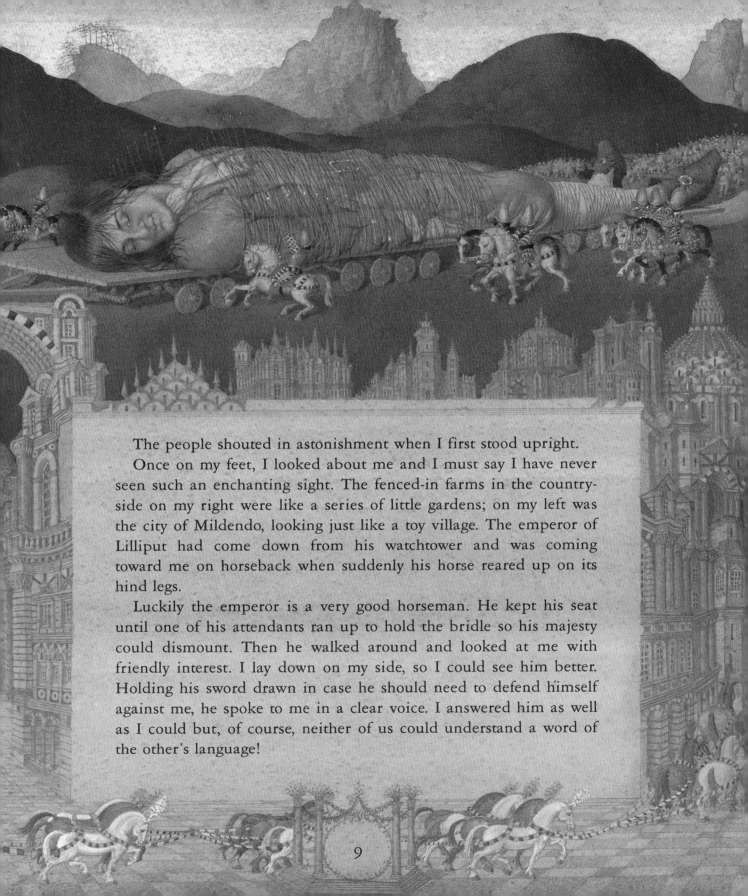

The people shouted in astonishment when I first stood upright.

Once on my feet, I looked about me and I must say I have never seen such an enchanting sight. The fenced-in farms in the country-side on my right were like a series of little gardens; on my left was the city of Mildendo, looking just like a toy village. The emperor of Lilliput had come down from his watchtower and was coming toward me on horseback when suddenly his horse reared up on its hind legs.

Luckily the emperor is a very good horseman. He kept his seat until one of his attendants ran up to hold the bridle so his majesty could dismount. Then he walked around and looked at me with friendly interest. I lay down on my side, so I could see him better. Holding his sword drawn in case he should need to defend himself against me, he spoke to me in a clear voice. I answered him as well as I could but, of course, neither of us could understand a word of the other's language!

After a while, the emperor and his courtiers departed. I was left with strong guards to protect me against those in the crowd who might try to harm me. In spite of the guards, some impudent ones shot arrows at me, one of which nearly hit me in the left eye. Six of these rascals were soon caught and tied up. Then the colonel had them handed over to me, to be punished as I saw fit. I took them all in my right hand, put five of them into my coat pocket and then, for a joke, pretended I was going to eat the sixth man! But I soon showed him he had nothing to fear, as I cut the strings he was tied up with and set him gently on the ground. Then I freed the others, too. I could see that the colonel and his soldiers were very pleased by my kindness.

That night and for the next two weeks or so I had to sleep, most uncomfortably, on the cold stone floor of the temple. But when the emperor realized this, he ordered a feather mattress made for me. Six hundred featherbeds of their usual size were sewn together to make a soft mattress for me. Sheets and blankets were made in the same way. They were pretty, like patchwork quilts, and I was glad to have them. Then three hundred tailors were hired to make me a suit of clothes in the Lilliputian style.

The emperor really seemed to want to be my friend. He persuaded his courtiers that I could be of great service to the country. He came to see me every day, and hired six of Lilliput's greatest scholars to teach me their language. Soon I was able to talk quite well. But, in spite of all the emperor's favors, I was still his prisoner. My left leg remained firmly chained to the wall of the temple. I begged the emperor to set me free, but he said I would have to be patient.

On one visit, the emperor brought with him two officers of the army, whom he ordered to search me. I could not very well refuse.

When the list of my possessions was read to the emperor he asked me to hand everything over to him. His tone was polite, as always— but three thousand of his soldiers surrounded me, with their bows and arrows ready to shoot if I did not obey! First I drew out my scimitar. When the sun flashed on its bright metal blade, the watching troops gave a shout between terror and surprise. Next I brought out what his inspectors had described as "two huge, hollow iron pillars."

These were, of course, my pistols. I loaded one pistol with gunpowder, but without bullets, so as to do no harm. Then I fired it into the air. Hundreds fainted and fell down as if they had been struck dead. Even the emperor was shaken. After this I gave him everything I had with me, except for my eyeglasses and a small telescope which I had managed to hide from his inspectors.

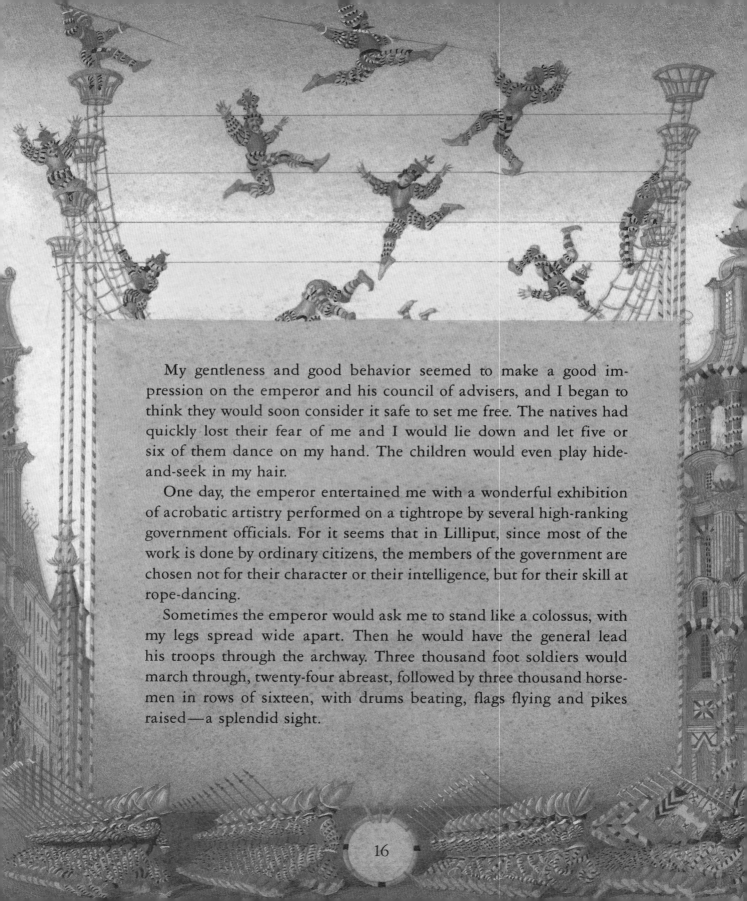

My gentleness and good behavior seemed to make a good impression on the emperor and his council of advisers, and I began to think they would soon consider it safe to set me free. The natives had quickly lost their fear of me and I would lie down and let five or six of them dance on my hand. The children would even play hide-and-seek in my hair.

One day, the emperor entertained me with a wonderful exhibition of acrobatic artistry performed on a tightrope by several high-ranking government officials. For it seems that in Lilliput, since most of the work is done by ordinary citizens, the members of the government are chosen not for their character or their intelligence, but for their skill at rope-dancing.

Sometimes the emperor would ask me to stand like a colossus, with my legs spread wide apart. Then he would have the general lead his troops through the archway. Three thousand foot soldiers would march through, twenty-four abreast, followed by three thousand horsemen in rows of sixteen, with drums beating, flags flying and pikes raised—a splendid sight.

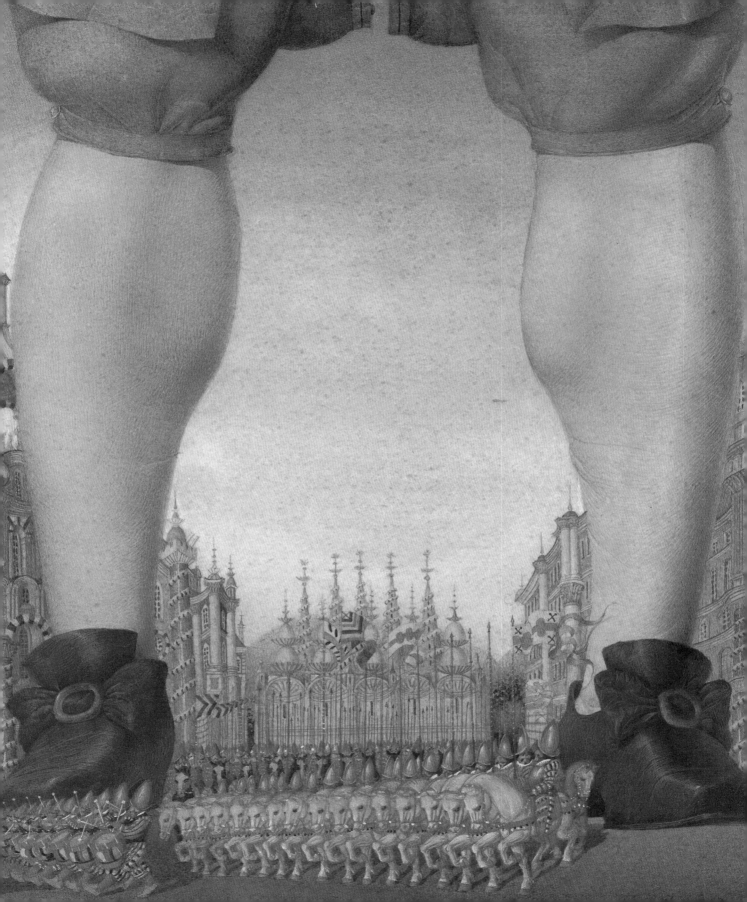

Finally my long-awaited independence day arrived! I was granted my liberty by vote of the emperor's council. Only one person had voted against it — Admiral Bolgolam. However, it was Bolgolam himself who brought me the good news. He also brought an official letter, which asked me to do certain things in return for being unchained. First, I was to make an exact survey of the entire country by walking around its borders. Second, I was not to leave the country without the emperor's permission. Third, I was to be Lilliput's ally against all enemies. I had to swear to all this in their way, which was to hold my right foot in my left hand, and place the middle finger of my right hand on the top of my head and the thumb on my ear.

With my new freedom, I could at last explore the city of Mildendo. Of course I had to be very careful not to step on any people or damage their houses. In the large park in the center of the city, I was able to lie down and look in at the windows of the royal palace. There, in a splendid room, the empress and the royal children and some ladies of the court were waiting to greet me. The empress graciously put her tiny hand out of the window for me to kiss.

All seemed to be going so well that I was shocked one night a few weeks later when a man named Reldresal, one of the emperor's councillors, came to see me unexpectedly. It was near midnight. Reldresal was clearly upset. "I want you to know," he said, "that we are in danger of an invasion from Blefescu, the other great power in the world. Blefescu's fleet is getting ready to attack us. The emperor asks for your help."

"Reldresal," I replied, "please assure the emperor that I would defend him and his country with my life if necessary."

And very soon I had made a plan. I would try to capture the enemy fleet by myself. The island empire of Blefescu was only about eight hundred yards away from the northeast coast of Lilliput. Lying down behind a hillock, I took out my pocket telescope and saw the Blefescan fleet at anchor in the harbor. There were over fifty men-of-war and many troop transports.

I asked for fifty stout iron bars, which I bent into hooks. Then I fastened to each a piece of strong rope. With these in hand, I waded into the water. I had to swim a little in the deeper parts but soon found my footing on the other side. When they saw me rising like a giant from the sea, the enemy sailors were so frightened that they leaped off their ships and swam to the shore.

There must have been thirty thousand little people lined up on the shore of Blefescu, including many men armed with bows and arrows. Hastily, I now began to fasten a hook to the prow of each Blefescan warship, but as I did this, the enemy archers sent thousands of arrows flying towards my hands and face. These were painful, and I would surely have lost my eyesight had I not remembered my eyeglasses, which I had hidden in my pocket. I put these firmly on my nose for protection, and went on with my work. Then, tying all the rope ends into a single knot, I began to pull. But, to my surprise, not a boat would move! They were *anchored*, of course! I had not thought of this. With my pocketknife I now had to cut each anchor chain, suffering many more arrow wounds, but finally I was able to pull all fifty warships away from the harbor with ease. The Blefescans screamed in grief and despair when they saw what was happening. Soon their emperor humbly admitted his defeat, and gave up his plans to invade Lilliput.

But now the emperor of Lilliput began dreaming of a bigger victory. He urged me to destroy the rest of the enemy fleet and to kill all who resisted. Worst of all, he wanted me to capture the emperor of Blefescu. He planned to make all the Blefescans slaves.

"Oh, no, your Majesty," I protested. "I could *never* be an instrument of bringing a free and brave people into slavery. You have defeated them, and they should be punished for their aggression—but not enslaved. What is called for now is a fair peace treaty."

The emperor seemed to be convinced by my words. A treaty between the two countries was agreed to, with many advantages to Lilliput, naturally. Because of my part in all this, I thought I would now be honored as a hero. But instead, I discovered that both Flimnap, the treasurer, and Admiral Bolgolam had taken my fairness to the Blefescans as a sign of disloyalty and had told the emperor that I was a traitor!

For a few weeks, however, everything seemed to have settled down again and the emperor and his entire family came often to visit me. They found it amusing to sit at a dining table set on top of my own and enjoy a banquet, while the royal guards rode around the edge of the table in carriages drawn by pairs of horses.

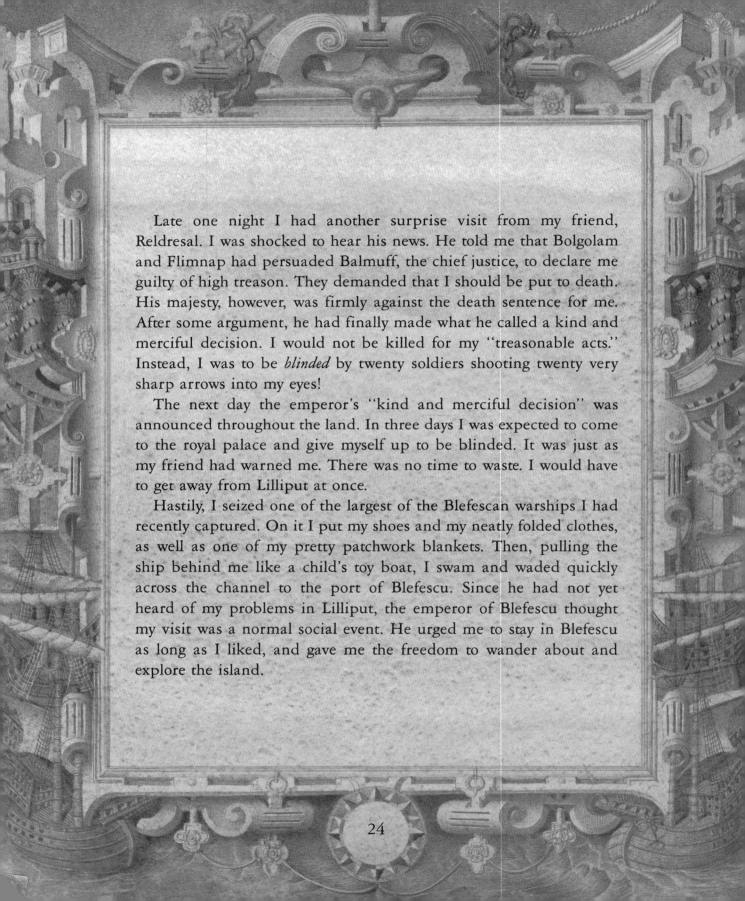

Late one night I had another surprise visit from my friend, Reldresal. I was shocked to hear his news. He told me that Bolgolam and Flimnap had persuaded Balmuff, the chief justice, to declare me guilty of high treason. They demanded that I should be put to death. His majesty, however, was firmly against the death sentence for me. After some argument, he had finally made what he called a kind and merciful decision. I would not be killed for my "treasonable acts." Instead, I was to be *blinded* by twenty soldiers shooting twenty very sharp arrows into my eyes!

The next day the emperor's "kind and merciful decision" was announced throughout the land. In three days I was expected to come to the royal palace and give myself up to be blinded. It was just as my friend had warned me. There was no time to waste. I would have to get away from Lilliput at once.

Hastily, I seized one of the largest of the Blefescan warships I had recently captured. On it I put my shoes and my neatly folded clothes, as well as one of my pretty patchwork blankets. Then, pulling the ship behind me like a child's toy boat, I swam and waded quickly across the channel to the port of Blefescu. Since he had not yet heard of my problems in Lilliput, the emperor of Blefescu thought my visit was a normal social event. He urged me to stay in Blefescu as long as I liked, and gave me the freedom to wander about and explore the island.

Not long after this, as I was walking alone on the far side of the island, I happened to see something floating near the shore. When I pulled it closer and turned it right side up, I found it was a boat, very seaworthy and in quite good condition! It must have been a lifeboat lost from some large ship. I carved out some clumsy paddles and made my way in it into the main port of Blefescu.

It seemed strange to me that there had been no word as yet from Lilliput about my escape. I learned later that the emperor had actually thought I would return in three days to obey his order to have my eyes put out. When the three days passed, and I did

not appear, he sent a messenger ordering the emperor of Blefescu to return me at once. Now, at last, he understood the danger I was in and promised to protect me.

By this time, however, I had learned not to count on the friendship of emperors. I decided to try to sail away by myself in the boat I had found. Hastily, I prepared to leave. In addition to my own supplies, I decided to take along six live Blefescan cows and four bulls and an equal number of rams and ewes and some food for all of these. I thought perhaps I could breed the tiny animals as pets when—or if—I got home.

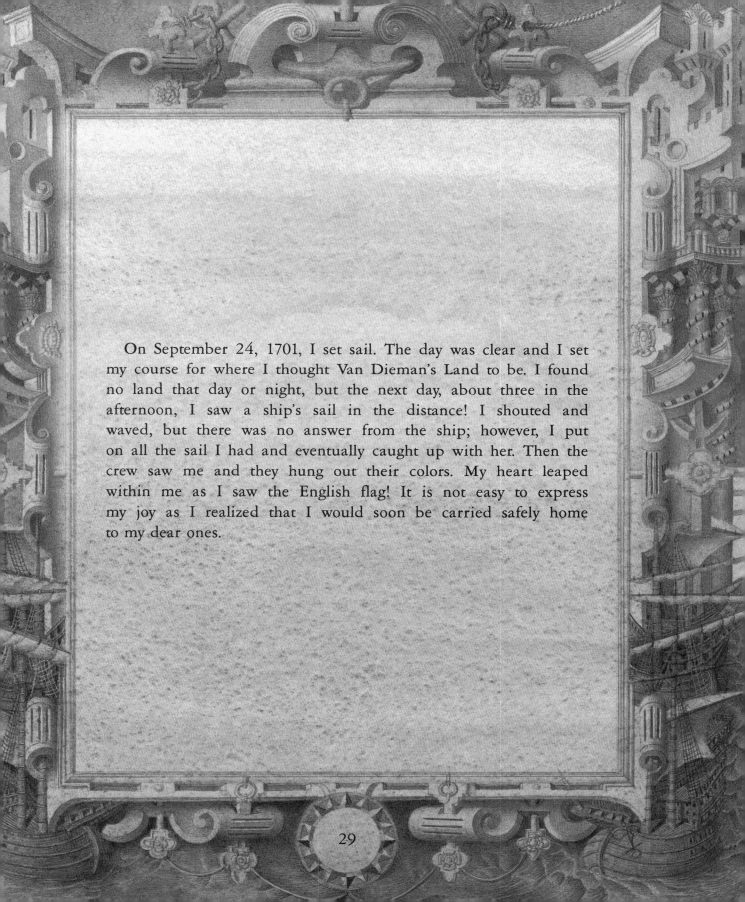

On September 24, 1701, I set sail. The day was clear and I set my course for where I thought Van Dieman's Land to be. I found no land that day or night, but the next day, about three in the afternoon, I saw a ship's sail in the distance! I shouted and waved, but there was no answer from the ship; however, I put on all the sail I had and eventually caught up with her. Then the crew saw me and they hung out their colors. My heart leaped within me as I saw the English flag! It is not easy to express my joy as I realized that I would soon be carried safely home to my dear ones.

The vessel that rescued me was an English merchantman, on its way back from Japan. The captain was a very pleasant fellow—but when I tried to tell him of my adventures he clearly thought my hardships had driven me a bit crazy. It was only when I brought out of my pocket my tiny cattle and sheep that he was convinced I was telling the truth.

Gulliver returned home on the 13th of April, 1702. He made a considerable fortune breeding and showing his Lilliputian sheep and cattle and was able to buy a fine new home for his family. However, before two months had passed, his love of travel led him once more to the sea. He embarked for the South Seas on the merchant ship *Adventure.* But that is another story...

About the Story

This book was planned as a first introduction for young readers to one of the most delightful fantasies in the English language. It is fervently hoped that this very much abbreviated version will inspire these same young readers, a few years hence, to read and savor the book in its entirety. In preparing the text, care was taken to preserve the period flavor and, where possible, the actual words of the original story, but many deliciously witty—or even hilarious—scenes had to be omitted here, to be enjoyed in the future. In the original work, entitled *Gulliver's Travels,* the hero journeys not only to Lilliput, but also to Brobdingnag (the land of the giants), to Laputa, to Glubbdubdrub (the island of sorcerers), and finally to the country of Houyhnhnms, a race of intelligent, noble horses served by the oddly humanlike Yahoos. Written primarily as political satire, it was readily understood as such by readers in Swift's time, who recognized his slyly exaggerated portraits of inept government and church leaders. But the secret of the story's enduring appeal lies in its framework of high adventure and imaginative fantasy, and the humor and charm with which it is told. Gulliver is Jonathan Swift, yes, but he is also Every Reader; intelligent, curious, idealistic, he is often shocked by the crass behavior of those he meets in his travels, yet he remains hopeful for the future and is always ready to embark on further adventures.

About the Author

Born in Ireland of English parents in 1667, Jonathan Swift graduated from Trinity College, Dublin. After several years in London as secretary to a distinguished Whig statesman and diplomat, he opted for a career in the priesthood rather than politics, though his interest in the latter remained keen. He was installed in 1713 as Dean of St. Patrick's Cathedral in Dublin, where he was nicknamed "The Gloomy Dean" for his strongly expressed and bitter social criticism. *Gulliver's Travels,* published in 1726, was really intended as a satire on the disturbed political scene in Britain. Swift died in 1742.

About the Artist

Gennady Spirin was born in a small city near Moscow in 1948, and graduated from the Strogonov Academy of Fine Arts. His beautiful illustrations, meticulously researched and exquisitely executed in pencil and watercolor, have brought him international renown and many distinguished awards. As a boy, his favorite book was *Gulliver's Travels,* and illustrating this beloved classic story has been the fulfillment of a lifelong dream.